My Name Is Elmo

By Constance Allen
Illustrated by Maggie Swanson

 A GOLDEN BOOK • NEW YORK

"Sesame Workshop,"® "Sesame Street,"® and associated characters, trademarks, and design elements are owned and licensed by Sesame Workshop. Copyright © 1993, 1997, 2013 by Sesame Workshop. All Rights Reserved. Published in the United States by Golden Books, an imprint of Random House Children's Books, a division of Random House, Inc., 1745 Broadway, New York, NY 10019, and in Canada by Random House of Canada Limited, Toronto, in conjunction with Sesame Workshop. Originally published in a different form in 1993. Published as a Little Golden Book with the title *Tickle Me, My Name Is Elmo* in 1997 by Golden Books Publishing Company, Inc., in conjunction with Sesame Workshop. A Golden Book, A Little Golden Book, the G colophon, and the distinctive gold spine are registered trademarks of Random House, Inc.
randomhouse.com/kids
SesameStreetBooks.com
www.sesamestreet.org
Educators and librarians, for a variety of teaching tools, visit us at RHTeachersLibrarians.com
ISBN 978-0-449-81066-8
Printed in the United States of America
10 9 8 7 6 5 4

Hello! Elmo is so happy to see you! Welcome to Sesame Street!

This is Elmo's room. See outside? There's Oscar's trash can. Hi, Oscar! And over there is Big Bird's nest. Hello, Big Bird!

See this hat? It's a firefighter's hat! Maybe when
Elmo grows up, Elmo will be a firefighter. Yeah!

This is Elmo's bed. This is Elmo's favorite teddy monster. And this is Elmo's favorite poster.

Do you want to make funny faces? Come on!
Let's make funny faces!

Did you know that furry little red monsters are
very ticklish? Tickle Elmo's toes!
Ha! Ha! Ha! That tickles!

Do you want to know Elmo's favorite color?
It's yellow! And blue! And red and pink and
green and orange and purple! Elmo likes all
colors. Yay!

This is Elmo's friend Ernie. Sometimes we play
horsie. Wheeeee! Giddyap, Ernie!

Elmo drew a picture. Do you want to see it?
Okay! Turn the page and you can see Elmo's
picture!

Here it is! See? Maybe Elmo will be a firefighter *and* an artist when he grows up.

Elmo will now show you a trick. Are you ready? Watch. Are you watching? Okay, Elmo will now bend over like this . . .

and everything will be upside down! See?
Now you try it.

This is Big Bird. We're friends. Sometimes we try to chase each other's shadows like this.

Here is one of Elmo's favorite games:

Here's Elmo's favorite number: 4. There are four letters in Elmo's name, and four wheels on Elmo's bike. Elmo has four toy cars. And Elmo's pet turtle, Walter, has four feet.

Elmo likes to meet new people. When he
meets them, this is what Elmo says. . . .

Hello! Elmo is so happy to meet you!